WILLDA the WITCH

Written by
ALEASHA REICH

Illustrated by
DEWITT STUDIOS

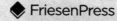

FriesenPress

Suite 300 - 990 Fort St
Victoria, BC, V8V 3K2
Canada

www.friesenpress.com

ISBN
978-1-03-910811-0 (Hardcover)
978-1-03-910810-3 (Paperback)
978-1-03-910812-7 (eBook)

1. JUVENILE FICTION, HOLIDAYS & CELEBRATIONS, HALLOWEEN

Distributed to the trade by The Ingram Book Company

This book is dedicated to
my favourite little humans.

Auntie Lee-Lee loves you always.

Willda the witch and her bunny, Pepper,
lived in a cottage that you could not see.

For the only entrance that existed was through the
hollowed-out oak of a tree.

It was there where she spent her days getting ready
for the very next Halloween.
She made candy and costumes to take into town,
so all of her work could be seen.

There was, however, an obstacle that
Willda never liked to tell.
She was very forgetful and if it wasn't for
this, she figured her life would be swell.

Today was a day she would not forget;
it was her favourite holiday—Halloween!
She made a list of things she had to do to
make sure her cottage was clean.

Now was the time to load up her broom
and take all of her goodies into town.
She made costumes for children who needed them;
a goblin, a witch, and a clown.

Willda and Pepper flew over the village,
dropping candy to the children below.
Willda's first two costumes were a hit,
and now it was Milly's turn for a show!
Things seemed to be perfect until she reached
into her bag and realized something. . . **OH, NO!**

The costume that Milly had hoped for
was absolutely nowhere in sight!
Willda wished that she didn't forget;
she was afraid she had ruined Milly's night.

Milly rushed to the door when she saw
Willda and her magical bunny outside.
Willda was so embarrassed to tell her the
truth that she hugged Milly and let out a sigh.

Milly picked up Pepper and she
did not even yell, shout or cry.
She exclaimed, "This could be the best
Halloween, would you both like to know why?"

Willda asked, "How can I save this night
and still make your costume a hit?"
Milly explained they just needed their
imaginations to make something else a great fit.

They jumped up and searched the house
together to see what they all could find.
A black tablecloth and some buttons, plus an
old kitchen broom that was one of a kind.

Willda picked up Pepper knowing that
he could grant the odd wish or spell.
She held him close to her heart and wished
Milly would like this new costume as well.

Milly jumped up and down while thanking
the two, her costume was made just right.
They smiled and realized Willda's memory
did not ruin that Halloween night.

Willda gasped as she looked at the clock,
realizing it was time to head home.
Pepper hopped to the door but something
was missing and he let out a very sad moan.

Willda knew right away why Pepper was
sad and she pointed at Milly's head.
She figured out a way to fix this problem
before any words were said.

"Sweet girl you need a hat is all,"
said Willda with a twinkle in her eye.
She took her own and placed it on Milly's
head before hopping on her broom to fly.

The two were now ready to take off
as they waved to Milly goodbye.
The moon was looking extra bright
as they flew toward the sky.

While Willda and Pepper watched
all of the trick or treaters below,
she realized it was ok to forget sometimes,
as Milly had shown her so.

CPSIA information can be obtained
at www.ICGtesting.com
Printed in the USA
BVHW020041080922
646549BV00005B/14

9 781039 108110